ANTONY
AND
CLEOPATRA

Written by William Shakespeare

Retold by John Dougherty

Illustrated by Alida Massari

CAST OF CHARACTERS

Cleopatra, Queen of Egypt

Octavius Caesar, adopted son of Julius Caesar, and a ruler of the Roman Republic

Mark Antony, ruler of the eastern Roman Republic

Enobarbus,
a trusted friend and
adviser to Mark Antony

Lepidus,
the third of the rulers of
the Roman Republic

Sextus Pompey,
son of Pompey the Great

Octavia,
Caesar's sister and
wife to Mark Antony

3

FOREWORD

The war between Julius Caesar and Pompey the Great was a fierce and bitter one, for each wanted to rule Rome. Leading their great armies, the two chased and fought one another across the known world until, in Egypt, Pompey was murdered.

Caesar returned to Rome in triumph. Now he was the most powerful man in the world – until he, too, was murdered, and Rome was left without a leader.

Caesar's best friend Mark Antony, his adopted son Octavius Caesar, and Lepidus, another friend of Caesar's, took power. They divided the Roman Republic between them, and Mark Antony took the east as his own.

Often, when the Romans conquered a country,
they would leave the king or queen on the throne.
That king or queen had to promise to serve Rome,
and rule their country as part of the Roman Republic.
One such queen was Cleopatra of Egypt, whose country
now fell under Mark Antony's rule.

But when Antony and Cleopatra met, they fell in love.
Soon neither was giving as much time to their duties
as they should …

1 MESSAGES FROM ROME

The messenger heard the soldiers grumbling as he entered the throne room.

"I think our general's lost his senses," one was saying. "Remember how his eyes used to glow with pride when he inspected his troops? Now he only has eyes for this Egyptian queen. He's the great Mark Antony, one of the three rulers of the world, but love's turned him into a fool."

The messenger bit his lip nervously as he knelt before Mark Antony. If what the soldiers were saying was true, his message wouldn't be welcome. Indeed, Antony barely looked at him. His eyes were fixed on Cleopatra, who sat by his side. "What is it?" he asked impatiently.

The messenger kept his head bowed.
"My lord, I've news from Rome."

"Maybe little Caesar Junior has an order for you,
Antony," Cleopatra teased. "Maybe he's going to tell you
to run home to Rome."

Antony bristled. He knew he should hear the message,
but he hated it when Cleopatra teased him. "I don't care
what Octavius says!" he said. "I'm staying here with you,
my love." He turned to the messenger. "Get out of here!
I don't want to hear your dull message." Taking Cleopatra
by the hand, he swept from the throne room, saying,
"Come on, my queen, let's find something fun to do."

"Does Antony think so little of Caesar?"
one of the soldiers muttered.

"He's not behaving like himself," the other said.

"I didn't believe the things people were saying
about him in Rome," said the first, "but it looks like
they're true. He's spending all his time with the queen.
He's completely ignoring his duties. And he's lost all
respect for Caesar."

The messenger frowned. This message
really mattered. He had to deliver it.

His chance came that evening. Antony couldn't stop wondering what the message might be, and Cleopatra could tell he was thinking about it.

Eventually she lost patience with him. "You're thinking about Rome, when you should be thinking about me!" she cried, storming away from him in a rage.

Moments later, the messenger appeared.

"Tell me your message," Antony said, more patiently than before.

"My lord," the messenger said, "I've bad news. Your brother Lucius turned against Caesar. He gathered an army, but Caesar beat them easily. Not only that – the army in Parthia have turned against Rome as well, and they've beaten our armies right across Asia, while …"

He stopped, afraid.

Antony smiled kindly at him. "I can guess what you've been told to say, and you're right. *'While Mark Antony's been spending all his time with Cleopatra.'* I think it's time I got back to work. Anything else? No? Then, thank you, and be on your way." As the messenger turned to go, Antony called, "Enobarbus!"

"My lord?" Enobarbus was Antony's most trusted friend and adviser, as well as a skilled soldier.

"We have to return to Rome," Antony told him.

Enobarbus frowned. "Her majesty Queen Cleopatra won't like it."

"I know, old friend, but we've stayed here too long already. I have duties to take care of, and I've been ignoring them. Besides this news I've just received, I've also heard that Pompey the Great's son, Sextus Pompey, has gathered a great navy. He's challenging Octavius Caesar to a battle at sea. Rome needs us."

Enobarbus was right. Cleopatra wasn't happy. She raged and pleaded and accused Antony of not caring for her. But Antony stood firm.

"I love you, Cleopatra," he said, "and my heart will stay here in Egypt with you – but Rome needs me."

And finally, Cleopatra sadly agreed that he should go.

2 CAESAR

"Look, Lepidus!" Octavius Caesar said angrily.
"I sent someone to Egypt to find out what Mark
Antony's doing, and here's the report. Antony's
spending all his time with Cleopatra. They go
fishing together; they go feasting together; they go
dancing together. He's ignoring all his duties!"

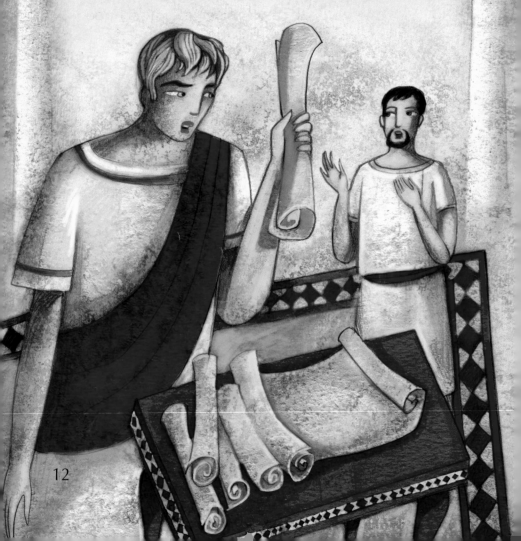

"Oh, but Caesar," Lepidus said, "you know what a good man Mark Antony is ..."

"You're too soft-hearted. If he's ignoring his duties, it means we have to do them as well as doing our own! It's not right, Lepidus, and I won't stand for it ..."

He was interrupted by the arrival of two messengers, one after the other. Both had clearly been hurrying and, by the looks on their faces, the news wasn't good.

"Lord Caesar," said the first, "Pompey's navy is growing stronger by the day! Many of the Roman people are taking his side against you."

"Not only that," the second added, "but Menecrates and Menas, the two famous pirates, have joined Pompey's side. They're capturing any ship that leaves our harbours!"

Caesar turned to Lepidus, slamming his fist against the table in fury. "You see? This is why we need Antony! He should be ashamed of himself. Instead of partying in Egypt, he should be in Rome where he's needed!"

"It's a shame," Lepidus agreed.

"Well, it looks as if Pompey's serious. We ought to start preparing for war."

Pompey and his new friends were also preparing for war.

"This will be easy," Pompey said, looking up. "The people love me, and my navy has control of the sea. Mark Antony's off feasting in Egypt, Caesar's losing followers, and nobody likes Lepidus."

"Perhaps," said Menas, "but Caesar and Lepidus are ready to fight, and they've gathered a mighty army."

Pompey frowned. "Rubbish," he said. "They're in Rome, waiting for Mark Antony to return – which he won't, because he'll never leave Cleopatra."

But just as he said this, a messenger entered, saluted, and said, "I bring news. Mark Antony's returning to Rome!"

Pompey's face fell. "This isn't good. Mark Antony's twice as good a soldier and general as the other two put together."

"True," said Menas, "but since Antony's brother turned against Caesar, I don't expect Caesar will be terribly pleased to see him."

"If they didn't have us to fight," Pompey said, "Antony, Caesar and Lepidus would all be fighting each other. They really don't like one another very much. But I suspect that fear of losing Rome to us will mean they'll put aside their arguments. Come on – we need to put together the strongest army we can."

Lepidus was nervous. He knew that of the three men who ruled Rome, he was the weakest. If either Octavius Caesar or Mark Antony turned on him, he'd be in trouble. Yet he was very much afraid that Caesar and Antony were going to argue once Antony arrived home. Both could be hot-headed, and if Antony heard some of the things Caesar had said about Cleopatra, it would cause problems.

So, as soon as Antony arrived in Rome to meet with Caesar, Lepidus went to find Antony's friend, Enobarbus.

"I know Antony listens to you, Enobarbus," he said, "and I know how wise you are. You'd really be doing him a favour if you asked him to speak calmly to Caesar."

Enobarbus wasn't fond of Lepidus. "I'll ask him to speak like himself," he said shortly.

"But now isn't the time for private arguments," Lepidus pleaded. "There are more important things to worry about!"

Enobarbus shrugged. "If Caesar brings up Antony's business, why shouldn't Antony talk about it?"

"Oh, please don't make things more difficult," Lepidus begged. "Look, here comes Antony now!"

"And there's Caesar," Enobarbus pointed out.

Lepidus forced his face into a smile. "My friends!" he said. "I know we've some difficult things to talk about, but let's speak kindly to each other. The most important thing is that we continue to rule Rome, after all."

"True," agreed Antony. "So, Caesar, I understand you're unhappy about my behaviour. What's it got to do with you, whether I stay in Egypt or not?"

"Nothing," said Caesar, "unless you're plotting with your Egyptian queen. Your brother led an army against me, after all."

"That had nothing to do with me!" Antony said.

"That's not all," said Caesar. "I sent you letters asking for help, and you didn't even read them! You promised to send me soldiers and weapons if I needed them, and then you broke your word!"

"I didn't mean to!" Antony said. "Your messenger gave me the letters when I was at a feast. I put them aside to read later and then forgot. For which I'm sorry."

"Well," said Enobarbus, "why don't you both pretend to be friends for now, and carry on arguing when you've beaten Pompey?"

"Be quiet," Mark Antony told him.

"No, he has a point," said Caesar. "You've really let me down, Antony, and I don't think we can ever truly be friends again. But I wish there was some way we could be more firmly joined as allies – some way you could prove to me that I can trust you."

At this, Agrippa, one of Caesar's advisers, stepped forward. "May I speak, Caesar?" he asked. At Caesar's nod, he went on: "If Mark Antony were to marry your half-sister, Octavia, you'd become brothers-in-law. You'd have to be friends, then."

"I don't think Cleopatra would be happy," Caesar said mockingly, watching Mark Antony's face.

Mark Antony thought quickly. He loved Cleopatra, but he loved power, too, and he didn't want to have to go to war against Caesar. This would be a good way to prevent that. And after all, it needn't be a real marriage. He could have the wedding ceremony, but not actually live with Octavia. Once Pompey was beaten, he could find a way to return to Egypt.

"I'm not married to Cleopatra," he said. "Very well. In order that we can be brothers, I'll marry Octavia. And then, knowing that we're joined as allies, let's deal with Pompey."

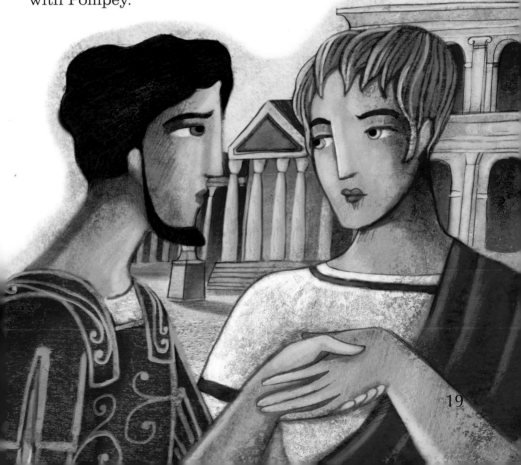

3 Peace talks and whispers

Only the most foolish general would have started a battle without first talking to his enemy to see if war could be avoided. So it was that Octavius Caesar, Mark Antony and Lepidus, along with their advisers, met with Pompey and his allies.

"Can we come to an agreement, Pompey?" Caesar asked. "It'll save a lot of lives."

"Well, I don't know," Pompey replied. "You took revenge against Brutus and Cassius when they killed your father, Julius Caesar. But my father died because your father made war against him. Why shouldn't I have my revenge for his death?"

"We're not frightened of your navy, Pompey,"
Mark Antony told him, "and our army is bigger
than yours."

"That's not really the point," Lepidus broke in, all
smiles and charm. "Please do tell us, Pompey, what
you think of our offer?"

"Yes, that's the main thing," Caesar agreed.

"Just to be clear," Pompey said, "your offer is this.
You'll give me Sicily and Sardinia. And in return,
you want me to rid the sea of pirates and give Rome
some of my stores of wheat. I'm tempted to accept but
I'm not sure I feel very happy with Mark Antony."
He turned to Antony, frowning. "Did you know that
when your brother was fighting with Caesar, your
mother came to me for help and I took her in?"

"I'd heard that, Pompey," Mark Antony broke
in quickly, "and I wanted to thank you. I owe you
a great deal for that."

Pompey studied Antony's face for a moment,
and then broke into a smile. "Well, then," he said,
"let's shake hands and be friends. I accept your offer.
We should celebrate! Allow me to invite you all aboard
my ship for a feast!"

But as they boarded the ship, the pirate Menas took
Pompey to one side. "Pompey," he whispered,
"how would you like to rule the world?"

"Whatever do you mean?"

"Look," Menas said, "these three share the world
between them. So once they're aboard and feasting,
let's sail out to sea and I'll kill them for you! Then you
can take everything that belongs to them!"

Pompey scowled. "You should have just done it
without saying anything," he said. "Then nobody could
have blamed me. But now you've suggested it, I can't
allow it. It would go against my sense of honour. I must
forbid you to harm my guests."

He marched ahead of Menas, who scowled at him
in turn. "Well," he muttered, too quietly for Pompey to
hear him, "if that's how you feel, don't be surprised if
I'm not here when you need me!"

It was a great feast,
and when it was over
and the peace agreement
with Pompey was signed,
Pompey sailed for Sicily.

Mark Antony, too, got
ready to leave for Athens,
taking Octavia with him.
He and Caesar parted like
the best of friends.

And in Egypt, Cleopatra, hearing the news of
Antony's marriage, almost killed the messenger.

4 PEACE IS BROKEN

Antony was furious. "Octavia, you won't believe what
your brother's done! He broke the agreement with
Pompey and declared war on him! Then as soon as he'd
beaten Pompey and had him killed, he arrested Lepidus!
Now Caesar's behaving as if he's the sole emperor
of Rome! He'll leave me no choice but to go to war with
him over this!"

Mark Antony's new bride looked worriedly
at her husband. "There must be some mistake, Antony.
Let me sail to Rome and talk to him. If you go to war
with my brother, I don't know what I'll do."

"Yes, of course," Antony answered. "Go as quickly
as you can, and see if you can sort this out."

Octavia hurried to prepare for her journey, not
knowing that Antony, too, was preparing to travel.
She left that day, on the fastest ship she could find.
It wasn't long before she was in Rome and appeared,
unannounced, before her brother.

"Octavia!" Caesar cried, leaping to his feet. "I'm so
sorry that your husband's treated you so badly!"

Octavia's brow wrinkled in puzzlement. "What do you
mean? He hasn't treated me badly at all! He was worried
by some reports he'd heard about you, so I told him I'd
come and talk to you, to put his mind at rest."

"And he was only too happy to let you come," Caesar
answered seriously, "so that he could go back to Egypt.
I'm sorry, sister, but he's tricked you. I've had people
watching him. He's clearly been planning this all along.
Almost as soon as you set sail for Rome, he returned
to Cleopatra. She's no longer angry with him, for
he's made her absolute ruler of Egypt, and he's given
her other parts of our empire, too. Now Antony and
Cleopatra are gathering an army to fight me."

Octavia's face fell. "Can this be true?"

"I'm afraid so," Caesar told her. "But all of Rome
loves you, and welcomes you. Only Antony, by running
back to Cleopatra, has betrayed you – and all of Rome.
And war will be the result."

26

Antony was indeed in Egypt, preparing for war,
and soon his chief adviser was arguing with Cleopatra.

"I'm telling you, Enobarbus," the queen said firmly,
"that I'll be taking part in the war."

Enobarbus wasn't happy. "But if you're there in
the battle, Antony will be worrying about you when he
should be concentrating on the fight!"

Cleopatra glared at him. "I'm ruler of Egypt,"
she said, "and I'll take part in the battle. Are you going
to argue with me?"

"No, your majesty," Enobarbus said quickly.
"I've said all I have to say. Anyway, here comes
the emperor."

Mark Antony entered the room, already in discussion with some of his other advisers. "We'll fight Caesar at sea, then," he was saying.

"Of course we'll fight at sea," Cleopatra agreed. "What else would we do?"

"But why?" Enobarbus asked.

"Because he's dared us to," Antony answered, as if this was obvious.

"But Caesar's crewmen are properly-trained sailors! Yours are just farmers who've never fought in a battle. And his ships are much better than yours."

"I've made up my mind," Antony insisted. "We'll fight him at sea."

Enobarbus shook his head, unable to believe Antony was being so foolish. "On land, you're the better general and you have the better army. At sea, all you can do is hope for good luck."

"I've got 60 ships," Cleopatra broke in. "They're all at least as good as Caesar's."

"There you are," said Antony, pleased. "Together, Cleopatra and I will fight Caesar at sea, and beat him. And even if we lose we can still fight him on land."

The preparations were made quickly, for Caesar's fleet was near. Leaving Enobarbus in charge of the army,

Antony and Cleopatra took command of their own fleets and sailed to meet the enemy. Mark Antony and Octavius Caesar were at war.

5 THE BATTLE

The fighting was fierce. Ships clashed together, smashing one another's oars into pieces. Catapults hurled great rocks into the sky, from where they came crashing down on the decks of their enemies. One ship slammed into another, armed men leaping across, their swords slashing and cutting. The sea was filled with the shouts of warriors and the sounds of war.

Enobarbus, watching from a hillside overlooking the sea, clenched his fists. He was still angry with Mark Antony for going into battle at sea – but it looked as if luck might be on his side. The fleets were more evenly matched than he'd feared. In fact, from up here, he could see that Mark Antony's forces seemed to be doing better than Caesar's …

But in the middle of the battle, Cleopatra couldn't see this. All she could see was the anger of the fighters, and the blood on the decks of her own ships. All she could hear was the roar of battle, the clashing of sword on sword, and the splintering of wood. And when a massive warship closed in on her own flagship, it was too much. Despite everything she'd said to Antony on land, at sea Cleopatra lost her nerve.

"Retreat!" she shouted at her captain.

"But ..." the captain began.

"*Retreat!*" Cleopatra shouted again, her eyes flashing.

The captain knew better than to argue with his queen. He gave the order to turn the ship away from the fight.

Up on the hillside, Enobarbus couldn't believe
his eyes. What was Cleopatra doing? She couldn't be
retreating ... she *was*! She was fleeing from the battle!
Torn by anger and despair, he watched helplessly as
the Egyptian flagship sailed away as fast as it could.
He knew what this would mean.

As he watched, Enobarbus's worst fears came true.
One by one, the other Egyptian captains saw their
queen retreating ... and one by one, they turned to
follow her. And then the worst thing of all happened.

Mark Antony saw that Cleopatra had fled.

As a soldier, he should have stayed with the fight. But Enobarbus had been right. Antony's heart was with Cleopatra, and when he saw her leaving the battle, his worst fear was that she'd be chased down by Caesar's fleet. So he, too, turned his ship and left the battle.

And without their commander, Mark Antony's fleet – like the battle – was lost.

6 Shame

By the time he returned to the Egyptian court, Mark
Antony couldn't believe what he'd done. Hot shame
burnt through him as he remembered how he'd ignored
Enobarbus's wise advice. Worse still, he'd fled from
the fight, leaving his men without a leader.

Before the battle, a third of the world had been his.
But now his fleet had been captured or destroyed.
His allies had turned their back on him, and many of
his soldiers had deserted him to join Caesar's army.
He was ruined.

Antony couldn't look at Cleopatra.

"Where have you led me?" he groaned. "My good name is gone, and my honour with it."

"Forgive my fearfulness, Antony!" Cleopatra sobbed. "I didn't know you'd follow me!"

"How could you not know?" Antony asked. "My heart's tied to you! Where you go, I have to follow!"

"I'm so sorry!"

"Now I'm in Caesar's power! I'll have to beg him to make peace. But ..." He finally looked at Cleopatra. "But of course I forgive you," he went on, his heart softening at the sight of her tear-streaked face. *I just hope,* he thought to himself, *that Caesar will be in a forgiving mood, too ...*

Caesar laughed when he saw Antony's messenger. "Not long ago," he chuckled, "Antony was so powerful that he'd send kings to carry his messages. Now he's sent one of Cleopatra's slaves!"

"Great Caesar," said the messenger, "I bring a message from Mark Antony."

"Go on," Caesar replied.

"Antony recognises you as his lord and ruler. He asks only that you might let him go on living in Egypt or, if not there, then in Athens. He asks for nothing more. Cleopatra also recognises your greatness. She offers Egypt to Rome once more, and asks only that she may continue to rule it in your name, and her children after her."

Caesar looked scornfully at him. "I'm not interested in what Antony wants," he said. "I'll listen to Cleopatra if she kills him, or at least has him thrown out of Egypt. Go and tell them both that."

Cleopatra was miserable. "Is this all my fault, Enobarbus? Or is it Antony's?"

Enobarbus was clear. "It's Antony's. So what if you were frightened and fled from Caesar's ships? He knew better than to leave the battle and follow you. Yet he chose to."

"He said *what*?" Antony's voice, loud and furious, entered the room a moment before he did. "Cleopatra, that *boy* Caesar says that he'll give you kingdoms if you send him my head!"

He turned to the messenger, who was coming nervously in behind him, and shouted, "Go back to Caesar and tell him this: anyone with your armies, your ships and your money could've won that battle! I challenge you to a fight – just you and me. My sword against yours." He led the reluctant messenger out.

Enobarbus shook his head. How could Antony be so foolish! First the sea battle, and now this. Caesar would never agree to fight him. He had too much to lose, and nothing to gain.

And, just at that moment, another messenger arrived from Caesar with a message full of sweet words for Cleopatra.

"Queen Cleopatra," the man said, "Caesar knows that you don't really love Antony. He knows that you're only on Antony's side because you're afraid of him."

"Caesar's very wise," said Cleopatra.

Enobarbus couldn't believe his ears. Was even Cleopatra turning on Antony now? He slipped out of the room, and went to find his master.

"Is there anything Caesar can do for you?" the messenger went on. "He'd be very happy to be able to help you. He'd be even happier if I could tell him that you'd left Antony and come over to Caesar's side."

Cleopatra smiled. "Kind messenger, you may tell Caesar that I kiss his conquering hand. I'll kneel at his feet and lay my crown there."

The messenger smiled. "A wise answer. And may I in turn kiss your hand?"

Cleopatra held out her hand and the messenger took it – just as Mark Antony entered the room with Enobarbus close behind.

"Who do you think you are?" Antony roared, crossing the room in three strides. "How dare you touch the queen?"

"Mark Antony!" the messenger began, his voice pleading.

40

Antony grabbed him and shoved him towards two servants. "Take him away!" he bellowed. "Whip him until he weeps, and then bring him back! I'll send him with a message for Caesar. And you!" He turned on Cleopatra. "Have you been deceiving me all this time? Were you lying when you said you loved me?"

"No! Antony, please – !" cried Cleopatra.

"What kind of fool have I been, putting my trust in you! Have the gods been laughing at me?"

"Why are you saying these things?" asked Cleopatra, her eyes full of tears, but Antony seemed to have run out of mercy. He stood over her, shouting, until the door opened once more and the servants threw the beaten messenger at Antony's feet.

Antony scowled at the man. "Go," he said. "Show yourself to Caesar, just as you are, and tell him that this is how angry he makes me. Then remind him that I've challenged him to face me – his sword against mine."

Caesar's answer came quickly: "My sword will not fight yours, Antony; but my army will battle what's left of your army. And since so many of your soldiers have joined me, tomorrow my army will win."

7 Defeat

The sky was just beginning to grow dawn-pink when Mark Antony buckled on his armour and called for Enobarbus to gather his troops for the battle.

Enobarbus didn't come.

Antony stopped a passing soldier. "You! Fetch me Enobarbus at once!"

The soldier looked oddly embarrassed. "Enobarbus isn't here, sir."

"I can see that! But he'll be somewhere around. Find him and bring him to me!"

The soldier looked anywhere but at his general. "Sir, I mean he's not in the camp. He's gone over to Caesar's side."

Once more shame flooded Mark Antony. He'd let his army down so badly that even his best friend no longer trusted him. He was lucky to have any soldiers left at all.

Yet he did have enough soldiers to make an army. And however ashamed he was of himself, and of the bad decisions he'd made out of love for Cleopatra, he was more angry with Caesar.

"Very well," he said. "We'll manage without Enobarbus. Tell the officers to gather their men. Today we defeat Caesar!"

Antony sounded more confident than he felt. If even Enobarbus had left him, could he believe that Cleopatra wouldn't?

The fighting was fierce that day. Even without the soldiers who'd deserted, Antony's army was stronger than Caesar had expected. By nightfall, Caesar's soldiers had been beaten back to their own camp. Antony celebrated that evening, but he knew the war was far from over.

The following day, Caesar once more attacked by sea. Antony's and Cleopatra's fleets sailed out to meet them. This time, Antony watched from the hillside where Enobarbus had stood, just days earlier, signalling his orders.

But as he watched, his heart sank. Both his own fleet and Cleopatra's, ignoring Antony's orders, sailed towards Caesar's fleet and surrendered. The battle – and the war – was over.

As her fleet was surrendering, Cleopatra was looking for Antony. It was unlikely now that he'd win, she thought, but not impossible. Perhaps, his forces would fight so well that Caesar would agree to end the war and divide the empire, or at least give Egypt to her and Antony.

But when she found him on the hillside, Antony was furious. "This is your fault!" he roared. "You've betrayed me to Caesar! You told your fleet to surrender, and they've persuaded mine to do the same! Get out of here before I kill you!"

In tears, Cleopatra fled. Her mind was a jumble of confusion. The war was lost. Perhaps Caesar would be kind? After all, that was why she'd pretended to his messenger that she was ready to surrender Antony and Egypt to him. But for Antony to believe this lie too, for him to think she'd betrayed him! How could she persuade him otherwise?

The idea that came to her was a desperate one, but it was all she could think of. Perhaps if Antony thought she was dead, he'd remember how much he loved her, and forgive her? Yes! He'd miss her, then! He'd feel bad that he'd said those cruel words to her. And when he discovered she was alive after all, he'd be so happy at the news that he'd forget his anger. She would send a messenger to tell him of her "death" at once.

Antony was still raging when the messenger found him. "Get out!" he roared. "Your queen betrayed me and she'll die for that."

The messenger's voice was quiet, and his face serious. "She's already dead, my lord."

The words hit Antony like a slap. The world seemed to have gone silent. "What did you say?"

"She's dead, my lord," the man repeated. "Her heart broke, and she died. Your name was the last word she said."

Antony felt suddenly weak. All his anger fell away, replaced by a dull ache. As the messenger left, he took off his armour.

"So," he said quietly, "this is how it ends. I've disgraced myself, and been defeated. Cleopatra's dead. Now Caesar will capture me, and march me in chains through the streets of Rome, where all my people will laugh at me. Then he'll kill me, or lock me in prison forever." Sadly, he drew his sword. "There's only one way to avoid that shame."

He pressed the point of the blade against his stomach and pushed, gasping as the blade went in.

As he lay in agony on the floor, another messenger arrived.

"Mark Antony!" he said, seeing the fallen general. "Cleopatra's not dead! She was suddenly afraid that you might do something foolish if you thought she was gone. She sent me to get you, but ... I'm too late!"

Antony nodded weakly. "Too late," he agreed. "Call my guards. Have them bring me to the queen."

They carried Antony to Cleopatra. The queen wept, to
see the man she loved so close to death. They whispered
to one another, and Cleopatra held Mark Antony's hand
until his heart fell still.

She was still weeping when Caesar's soldiers came
for her. Not wanting to be taken prisoner, she seized
a dagger, but the soldiers snatched it from her hand
and dragged her before the emperor.

"Cleopatra," Caesar said, smiling, "although you're my prisoner, I'll treat you as my friend. You may send your servants to fetch you anything you want. But if you try again to take your own life, you'll be punished. You're coming back to Rome with me, and I'll show you to the people to prove that I've conquered Egypt."

Cleopatra bowed her head, as if obeying Caesar. She settled herself in the room that he gave her; then she sent her servants out to find the comforts she wanted.

Before long, one of Caesar's soldiers entered. "There's a farmer outside. He's brought you the basket of figs you sent for."

"Let him come in," Cleopatra said, and the farmer entered and gave her the basket.

As soon as Cleopatra was alone, she called for her servants. "Bring me my robe and crown!" she ordered.

They dressed her so that she looked as royal as the day that Mark Antony fell in love with her. Then she reached into the basket and, from underneath the figs, she took out the snake that – at her order – the farmer had hidden there. Tenderly she stroked it, and then she pushed it hard against her chest.

The snake, terrified, bit deep.

Cleopatra lay back on her bed, feeling the snake's venom burning through her veins.

Now Caesar would never parade her before the people of Rome. She'd be remembered as the most noble queen of Egypt, not as a prisoner in chains. And her love for Mark Antony, and his love for her, would be remembered forever.

Cleopatra closed her eyes, whispered Antony's name, and breathed no more.

CLEOPATRA

Ideas for reading
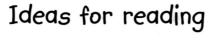

Written by Clare Dowdall, PhD
Lecturer and Primary Literacy Consultant

Reading objectives
- identify and discuss themes and conventions in and across a wide range of writing
- check that the book makes sense to them, discussing their understanding and exploring the meaning of words in context
- discuss and evaluate how authors use language, including figurative language, considering the impact on the reader

Spoken language objectives:
- participate in discussions, presentations, performances, role play, improvisations and debates

Curriculum links: History – Roman Empire

Resources: ICT for research; pens and paper; digital camera

Build a context for reading
- Look at the front cover together. Ask children to describe what they can see and what they think the story's about.
- Read the blurb together. Discuss what the figurative language means, and how this makes the reader feel, e.g. "Mark Antony … is torn" and "his head belongs to Rome".
- Discuss what the words "tragedy" and "triumph" mean, and ask for examples of triumph and tragedy from the children's own experiences.

Understand and apply reading strategies
- Look at the cast list on pp2–3, and help children to read the names. Sketch a web to show how the characters are related.
- Ask for a volunteer to read the foreword. Ask children questions about the events described to check and develop their understanding.